Book Club Edition

First American Edition. Copyright © 1980 by Walt Disney Productions.
All rights reserved under International and Pan-American Copyright
Conventions. Published in the United States by Random House, Inc.,
New York, and simultaneously in Canada by Random House of Canada
Limited, Toronto. Originally published in Denmark as ALADDIN OG
GULNARE by Gutenberghus Gruppen.
ISBN: 0-394-84782-2 (trade); 0-394-94782-7 (lib. bdg.)
Manufactured in the United States of America
4 5 6 7 8 9 0   B C D E F G H I J K

WALT DISNEY PRODUCTIONS
presents

ALADDIN
and the Sly Magician

Random House 🏠 New York

Aladdin was married to a lovely princess.
They lived in a big palace.

It belonged to the princess's father,
the rich sultan.

The palace had a beautiful garden.
Aladdin and the princess liked to
visit the garden.

The palace had horse stables, too.
The princess liked to watch Aladdin
ride his horse.

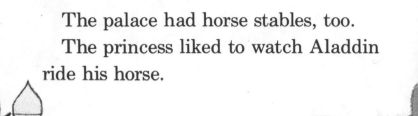

And she liked to listen to Aladdin's songs.
Her favorite song was about Aladdin when
he was a poor boy.

There once was a sly
magician who knew
about a magic lamp.
It was in a cave.

The cave door
closed while Aladdin
was still inside!

Aladdin was scared
in that cave!

Then he rubbed
the lamp.

A genie appeared.

"Make a wish,"
said the genie.

"I wish to escape,"
said Aladdin.

POOF! He was
home!

He paid Aladdin
to bring him the
lamp.

But poor Aladdin!
He did not have
enough time to get
out of the cave.

Next, Aladdin wished to marry the sultan's daughter.

His wish was granted.

Then he wished for gold.

Soon he had so much that he did not need to use the lamp anymore.

Aladdin nearly forgot about the sly magician.

But the sly magician did not
forget about Aladdin.

He wanted his lamp back!

One day in the market, the sly magician heard some men talking.

They spoke about the rich young Aladdin.

"Aladdin has my lamp," he said to himself. "I bet he asked the genie for gold!"

"I must get my lamp back," the magician said to himself.

The magician had a plan.
He dressed like a merchant.
He set up his tent near the palace.

The next morning Aladdin went for a ride.

In a minute Aladdin was out of sight.
The sly magician walked over to the
palace courtyard.

He opened a sack filled with lamps.
"New lamps for old, new lamps for
old," he cried.

Many people traded their old lamps
for shiny new ones.

One of Aladdin's servants heard the
sly magician's cry.

She ran upstairs quickly.
She got Aladdin's lamp.
How pretty a shiny new
lamp will be, she thought.

The servant gave the magician the rusty old lamp.

He gave her a shiny one in return.

The sly magician was very happy.

He ran to his tent as fast as he could.
"Aha! Now the genie will grant *my* wishes,"
he said, rubbing the lamp.

POOF!

There was the genie.

"What can I do for you, Master?"
the genie asked.

"Move Aladdin's palace
to a faraway place!"
the magician said.

PRESTO!
The palace was gone.
A big hole was left in the garden.

Later that morning, Aladdin returned
from his ride.

The sultan ran over to him.
"Look what happened!" he cried.
"The palace is gone. And the
princess is gone too!"

Poor Aladdin was miserable.

I *must* find out what happened, he thought.

Aladdin walked around
the market.

People there told Aladdin how
the merchant had cried out,
"New lamps for old!"

Aladdin figured out what
had happened.

"The sly magician got the lamp,"
said Aladdin sadly.

Suddenly Aladdin
remembered a medal he
had found in the cave.
He had never used it.

"Maybe this is magic,
too," he said.
He rubbed it gently.

POOF!
A new genie
appeared!

"What can I
do for you?"
the genie asked.

"Please return the princess and the palace," said Aladdin.

"I do not have the power to move the princess or the palace," said the genie. "But I can take you to them."

POOF!

In a minute Aladdin was at the
palace.

The first person Aladdin saw was
his own guard.

"Where is the princess?"
asked Aladdin.

Aladdin found her in
the kitchen.
She was working as
a maid.

"How happy I am to see you!"
they both said.

"Do you know where the sly magician
hid the lamp?" asked Aladdin.

"In his bag," said the princess.

"Hmm," said
Aladdin.
"We will take
it from him.
I have a
plan."

Aladdin ran to a shop in town.
He bought what he needed for his plan.

The princess served the sly magician his tea.

But first Aladdin dropped a sleeping potion into the tea.

Soon the magician's head nodded.
He was fast asleep!
Aladdin snuck into the room.
Quickly he took the lamp from the
magician's bag!

Aladdin rubbed
the lamp.
  And there was
the first genie!
  "What can
I do for you,
Master?" he said.

"Take us home! Take the
palace home too!" Aladdin
commanded.

PRESTO!

The beautiful palace was back where
it belonged.

Aladdin and his princess were safely
home, too.

Aladdin and the princess gave a big party.
They told everyone about the sly magician.
Everyone agreed never to let him into the
kingdom again.

Aladdin put the lamp in a special place.
A guard watched it day and night.

Aladdin and the princess felt very safe...
and very, very happy.